Block City

Robert Louis Stevenson
Illustrated by Daniel Kirk

Simon & Schuster Books for Young Readers
New York   London   Toronto   Sydney

SIMON & SCHUSTER BOOKS FOR YOUNG READERS
An imprint of Simon & Schuster Children's Publishing Division
1230 Avenue of the Americas, New York, New York 10020
Illustrations copyright © 2005 by Daniel Kirk
SIMON & SCHUSTER BOOKS FOR YOUNG READERS is a trademark of Simon & Schuster, Inc.
Book design by Lucy Ruth Cummins
The text for this book is set in Triplex Serif.
The illustrations for this book are rendered in Prismacolor pencils
over Windsor and Newton gouache on Arches paper.
Manufactured in China
16 18 20 19 17 15
CIP data for this book is available from the Library of Congress.
ISBN 978-0-689-86964-8
0923 SCP

**In case you didn't know, the word "kirk" means church.
You can trust me on this one—Daniel Kirk**

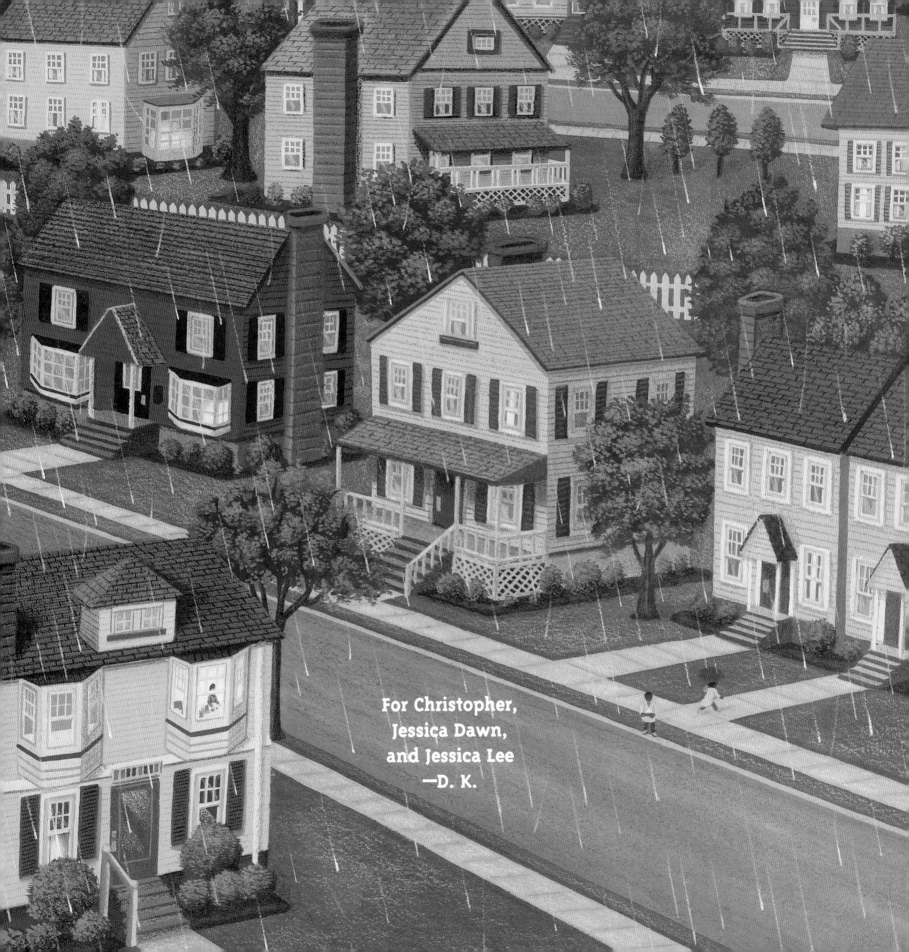

For Christopher,
Jessica Dawn,
and Jessica Lee
—D. K.

What are you able
to build with your blocks?

Castles and palaces,
temples and docks.

Rain may keep raining,
and others go roam,

But I can be happy
and building at home.

Let the sofa be mountains,
the carpet be sea,

There I'll establish
a city for me:

A kirk and a mill
and a palace beside,

And a harbor as well
where my vessels may ride.

Great is the palace
with pillar and wall,

A sort of a tower
on the top of it all,

And steps coming down
in an orderly way

To where my toy vessels
lie safe in the bay.

This one is sailing
and that one is moored:

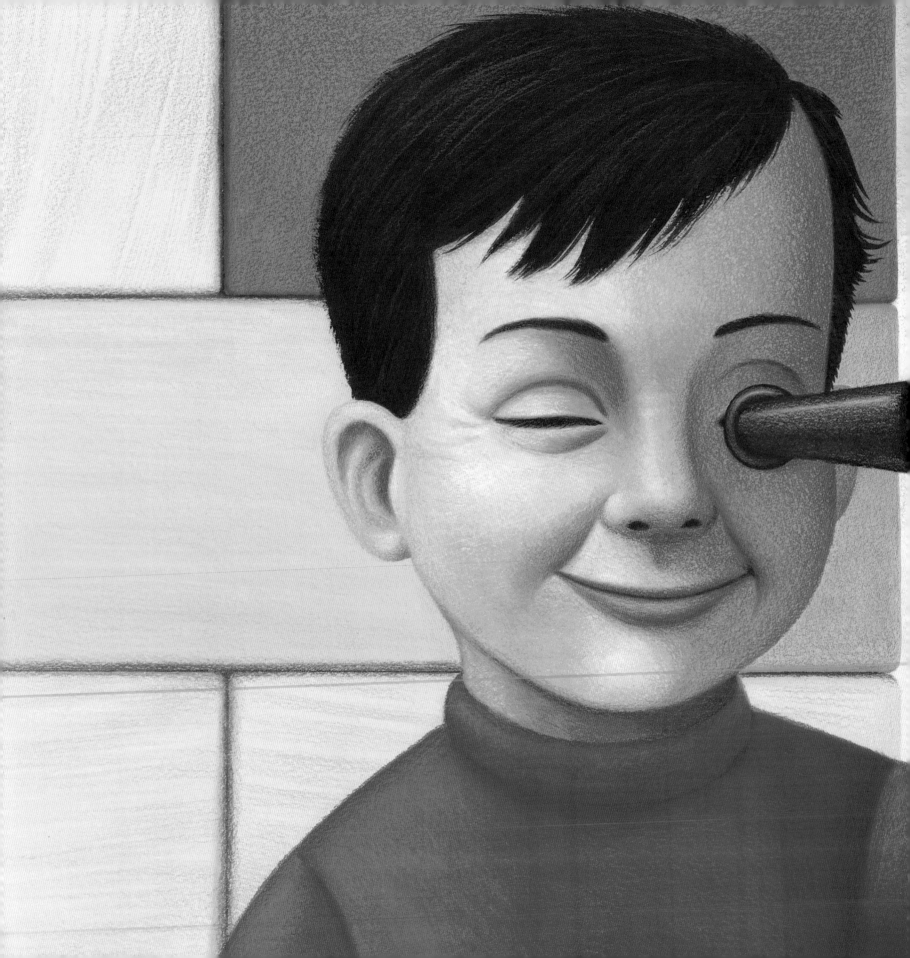

Hark to the song
of the sailors onboard!

And see on the steps
of my palace, the kings

Coming and going
with presents and things!

Now I have done with it,
down let it go!

All in a moment
the town is laid low.

**Block upon block
lying scattered and free,**

What is there left
of my town by the sea?

Yet as I saw it,
I see it again,

The kirk and the palace,
the ships and the men,

And as long as I live
and where'er I may be,

I'll always remember . . .

my town by the sea.